THIRSTY ROOTS

By NADIA HIGGINS
Illustrations by CHRIS BIGGIN
Music by DREW TEMPERANTE

CANTATA LEARNING

WWW.CANTATALEARNING.COM

CANTATA
LEARNING

Published by Cantata Learning
1710 Roe Crest Drive
North Mankato, MN 56003
www.cantatalearning.com

A note to educators and librarians from the publisher: Cantata Learning has provided the following data to assist in book processing and suggested use of Cantata Learning product.

Publisher's Cataloging-in-Publication Data
Prepared by Librarian Consultant: Ann-Marie Begnaud
Library of Congress Control Number: 2016938081
Thirsty Roots
Series: My First Science Songs
By Nadia Higgins
Illustrations by Chris Biggin
Music by Drew Temperante
Summary: Learn how roots help plants soak up water and get nutrients in this illustrated story set to music.
ISBN: 978-1-63290-790-5 (library binding/CD)
ISBN: 978-1-68410-113-9 (paperback)
Suggested Dewey and Subject Headings:
Dewey: E 575.54
LCSH Subject Headings: Roots (Botany) – Juvenile literature. | Roots (Botany) – Songs and music – Texts. | Roots (Botany) Juvenile sound recordings.
Sears Subject Headings: Plants – Anatomy. | School songbooks. | Children's songs. | Popular music.
BISAC Subject Headings: JUVENILE NONFICTION / Science & Nature / Botany. | JUVENILE NONFICTION / Music / Songbooks. | JUVENILE NONFICTION / Science & Nature / Flowers & Plants.

Book design and art direction: Tim Palin Creative
Editorial direction: Flat Sole Studio
Music direction: Elizabeth Draper
Music written and produced by Drew Temperante

Printed in the United States of America in North Mankato, Minnesota.
072017 0367CGF17

ACCESS THE MUSIC!
SCAN CODE WITH MOBILE APP
CANTATALEARNING.COM

TIPS TO SUPPORT LITERACY AT HOME

WHY READING AND SINGING WITH YOUR CHILD IS SO IMPORTANT

Daily reading with your child leads to increased academic achievement. Music and songs, specifically rhyming songs, are a fun and easy way to build early literacy and language development. Music skills correlate significantly with both phonological awareness and reading development. Singing helps build vocabulary and speech development. And reading and appreciating music together is a wonderful way to strengthen your relationship.

READ AND SING EVERY DAY!

TIPS FOR USING CANTATA LEARNING BOOKS AND SONGS DURING YOUR DAILY STORY TIME

1. As you sing and read, point out the different words on the page that rhyme. Suggest other words that rhyme.
2. Memorize simple rhymes such as Itsy Bitsy Spider and sing them together. This encourages comprehension skills and early literacy skills.
3. Use the questions in the back of each book to guide your singing and storytelling.
4. Read the included sheet music with your child while you listen to the song. How do the music notes correlate to the words of the song?
5. Sing along on the go and at home. Access music by scanning the QR code on each Cantata book. You can also stream or download the music for free to your computer, smartphone, or mobile device.

Devoting time to daily reading shows that you are available for your child. Together, you are building language, literacy, and listening skills.

Have fun reading and singing!

Plants are all around us, but there is more to them than what we see. Under the ground, they have roots. Roots hold plants in place. They take in water and **nutrients** that plants need to grow.

To learn more about thirsty roots, turn the page and sing along!

One, two, three, four, five, six!

Six plant parts and they go like this:
roots, stems, leaves,
flowers, fruit, and seeds!

Each part plays a special role.
Roots help plants grow and grow.

Under the ground, day after day,
roots keep plants from blowing away.

But that's just one part of what roots do.
Roots have a job that might surprise you.

Roots are thirsty. Did you know?
They soak up water all day long.

And in that water, nutrients flow,
keeping plants healthy and strong.

School Garden

Dig in the soil. Pull up some roots.
Sort them into two main groups.

Some are thick, growing straight down.
Others branch out all around.

Roots are thirsty. Did you know?
They soak up water all day long.

And in that water, nutrients flow,
keeping plants healthy and strong.

Calling one, calling all,
everybody do the root crawl!

Spread those roots out, down, down, down.
Anchor that plant deep in the ground.

Soak up water—nutrients, too.
Come on, thirsty roots! Show us your moves!

Carrots are roots, crunchy and sweet.
What other roots are good to eat?

Turnips, beets, and **rutabagas**,
radishes, and sweet potatoes.

Beet
Radish
Carrot
turnip
Rutabaga
Sweet
Potato

Roots are thirsty. Did you know?
They soak up water all day long.

And in that water, nutrients flow,
keeping plants healthy and strong.

SONG LYRICS
Thirsty Roots

One, two, three, four, five, six!
Six plant parts and they go like this:
roots, stems, leaves,
flowers, fruit, and seeds!

Each part plays a special role.
Roots help plants grow and grow.

Under the ground, day after day,
roots keep plants from blowing away.
But that's just one part of what roots do.
Roots have a job that might surprise you.

Roots are thirsty. Did you know?
They soak up water all day long.
And in that water, nutrients flow,
keeping plants healthy and strong.

Dig in the soil. Pull up some roots.
Sort them into two main groups.
Some are thick, growing straight down.
Others branch out, all around.

Roots are thirsty. Did you know?
They soak up water all day long.
And in that water, nutrients flow,
keeping plants healthy and strong.

Calling one, calling all,
everybody do the root crawl!
Spread those roots out, down, down, down.
Anchor that plant deep in the ground.
Soak up water—nutrients, too.
Come on, thirsty roots! Show us your moves!

Carrots are roots, crunchy and sweet.
What other roots are good to eat?
Turnips, beets, and rutabagas,
radishes, and sweet potatoes.

Roots are thirsty. Did you know?
They soak up water all day long.
And in that water, nutrients flow,
keeping plants healthy and strong.

Thirsty Roots

Hip Hop
Drew Temperante

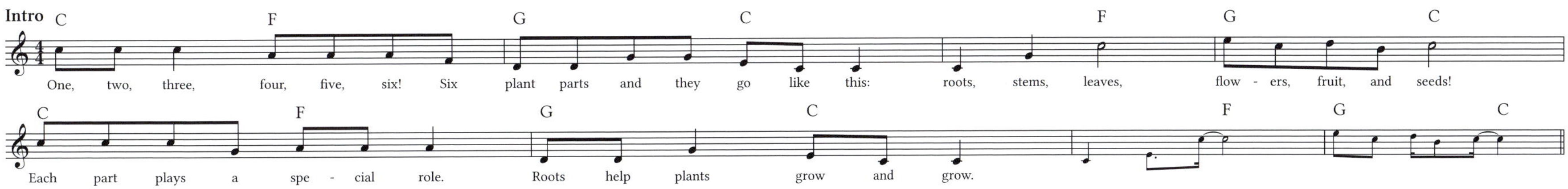

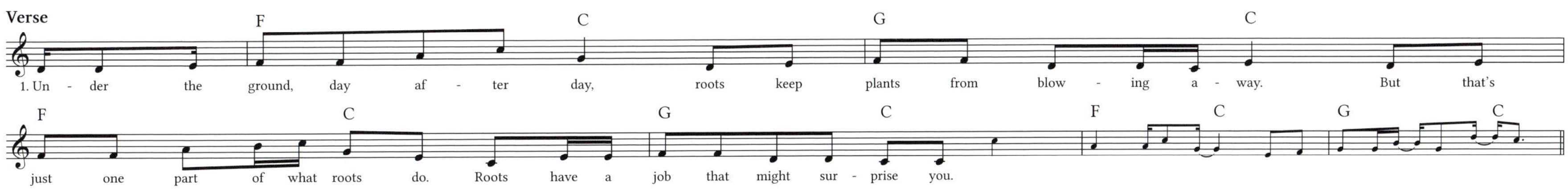

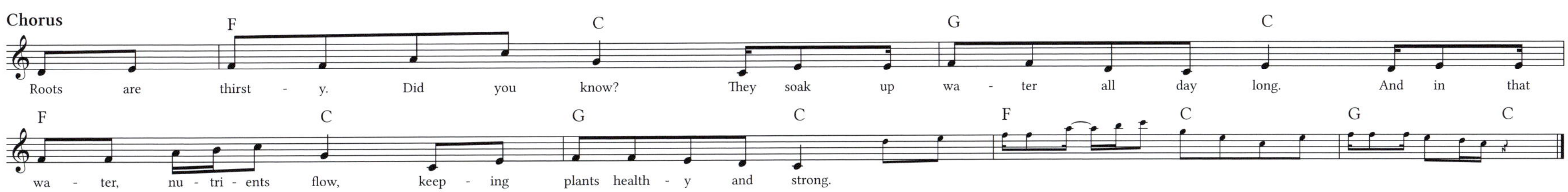

Verse 2
Dig in the soil. Pull up some roots.
Sort them into two main groups.
Some are thick, growing straight down.
Others branch out, all around.

Chorus

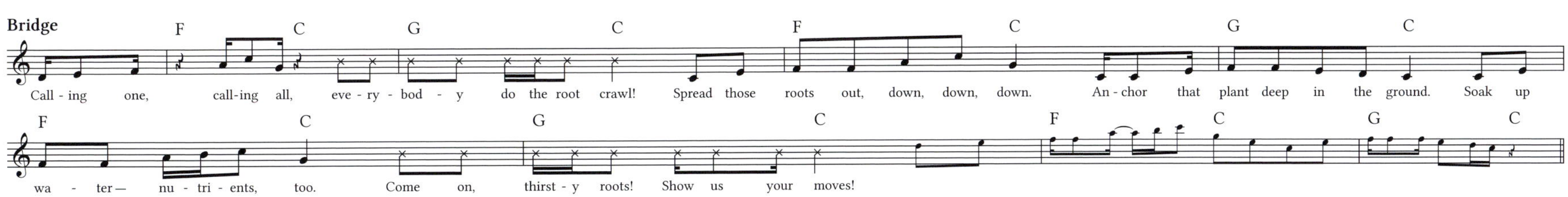

Verse 3
Carrots are roots, crunchy and sweet.
What other roots are good to eat?
Turnips, beets, and rutabagas,
radishes, and sweet potatoes.

Chorus

GLOSSARY

anchor—to keep something firmly in place

nutrients—substances people, animals, and plants need to live and grow

rutabagas—large yellowish root vegetables

turnips—round yellow or white root vegetables

GUIDED READING ACTIVITIES

1. Draw a picture of a tree. Underneath it, draw what you think its roots would look like.

2. Go outside with an adult who can help you find a weed or some other plant that isn't needed. Pull it up and look at its roots.

3. This book showed you many kinds of root vegetables that are good to eat. Which one is your favorite? What other root vegetables do you like to eat?

TO LEARN MORE

Aloian, Molly. *What Are Bulbs and Roots?* New York: Crabtree, 2012.

Bishop, Celeste. *Why Do Plants Have Roots?* New York: PowerKids, 2016.

Higgins, Nadia. *Experiment with a Plant's Roots*. Minneapolis: Lerner, 2015.

Throp, Claire. *All about Roots*. Chicago: Capstone Heinemann Library, 2015.